When Lightning Comes in a Jar

When Lightning

For my two beloved children,
Traci Denise and Steven John.
Tell your children about how you caught lightning in
a jar.

PATRICIA LEE GAUCH, EDITOR

PUFFIN BOOKS
Published by the Penguin Group
Penguin Young Readers Group, 345 Hudson Street, New York, New York 10014, U.S.A.
Penguin Group (Canada), 90 Eglinton Avenue East, Suite 700, Toronto, Ontario, Canada M4P 2Y3
(a division of Pearson Penguin Canada Inc.)
Penguin Books Ltd, 80 Strand, London WC2R 0RL, England
Penguin Ireland, 25 St Stephen's Green, Dublin 2, Ireland
(a division of Penguin Books Ltd)
Penguin Group (Australia), 250 Camberwell Road, Camberwell, Victoria 3124, Australia
(a division of Pearson Australia Group Pty Ltd)
Penguin Books India Pvt Ltd, 11 Community Centre, Panchsheel Park, New Delhi - 110 017, India
Penguin Group (NZ), Cnr Airborne and Rosedale Roads, Albany, Auckland 1310, New Zealand
(a division of Pearson New Zealand Ltd)
Penguin Books (South Africa) (Pty) Ltd, 24 Sturdee Avenue, Rosebank, Johannesburg 2196, South Africa

Registered Offices: Penguin Books Ltd, 80 Strand, London WC2R 0RL, England

First published in the United States of America by Philomel Books,
a division of Penguin Young Readers Group, 2002
Published by Puffin Books, a division of Penguin Young Readers Group, 2007

10 9 8 7 6 5 4 3
Copyright © Babushka Inc., 2002
All rights reserved

THE LIBRARY OF CONGRESS HAS CATALOGED THE PHILOMEL BOOKS EDITION AS FOLLOWS:
Polacco, Patricia.
When lightning comes in a jar / Patricia Polacco.
p. cm.
Summary: A young girl describes the family reunion at her grandmother's house, from the food
and baseball and photos to the flickering fireflies on the lawn.
ISBN: 0-399-23164-1 (hardcover)
[1. Family reunions—Fiction. 2. Grandmothers—Fiction. 3. Family life—Fiction.] I. Title.
PZ7.P75186 Wh 2002 [Fic]—dc21 2001045925
Puffin Books ISBN 978-0-14-240350-1
Manufactured in China

The text is set in 16-point Adobe Jenson. The illustrations are rendered in watercolor and pencil.

Comes in a Jar

PATRICIA POLACCO

PUFFIN BOOKS

Today is my family reunion! I can hardly wait. My dad's side of the family will come soon. It's been ages since I've seen them all. Before, our reunions were always at my gramma's house, but this year it is going to be at mine! I'm so anxious to see my cousins—especially Lydia and Sandy! They will be wearing the same colors that we always wear at family reunions. They wore them at our last reunion!

How I remember *that* day. Gramma and I stood in her front window, waiting for my relatives to come.

"I can't wait to see them all," I said to her.

"I know," she answered.

"Will there be Jell-O like there always is?" I asked.

"Yes," she answered.

"And baseball and croquet like there always is?"

"And bag races, too."

"And will you tell stories like you always do?"

"Might," Gramma said, looking up at the sky. "And we might catch lightning in a jar."

"Lightning in a jar?" I asked . . . this was new.

And then my relatives started driving up by the carload. One after another. Finally, the car I was waiting for rolled up and my five cousins piled out—Sandy, Freddie, Billy, Lydia and Karl!

Sandy, Lydia and I squealed and ran for the porch swing, just like we always did. We held hands and pushed the swing with our bare feet. We told secrets that we had kept for a whole year.

I told them about the lightning in a jar.

When my dad called out, "Who's going to help unload these baskets from the car?" we shouted, "We will!" and we lugged baskets full and heavy to the tables in the maple grove.

"Wonder how many Jell-O salads there will be?" my cousin Freddie asked.

"Gazillions. There always are," my cousin Billy answered.

Sure enough, there were gazillions. They jumped and shook every time we bumped the table. They seemed alive.

"Bet there'll be as many meatloafs, too," my brother chimed in.

There they were as we unpacked them—zillions of meatloafs. They were all different, too. Each auntie had her own recipe, including Aunt Bertha, who made one with a hard-boiled egg in the middle. When we cut it, there was a perfect slice of egg. Like a giant eye.

Our aunties and Gramma flitted around the tables like butterflies going from flower to flower. They perked up the lettuces, or rearranged the tomatoes and set slices of meatloaf so they looked perfect.

When Gramma and the aunties took off their aprons, we all knew it was time to gather at the table. We all held hands. Uncle Weyland said the blessing. Then everyone sat down and dove into the food, piling it high on their plates. Some as high as haystacks!

My brother, Richie, was sitting with some older girls that came with our older cousins. He was acting silly. I could tell he liked one of them. Embarrassing!

When we thought we couldn't eat any more, Gramma and my aunties put their aprons back on and started getting all of the pies and cakes from the kitchen.

There was something magical about my gramma and her sisters this day, like they knew something they weren't telling. I did wonder how Gramma was going to catch lightning in a jar, and every so often I'd stop her and ask her how.

She'd just smile and say, "Easy. Someday you'll do it, too."

After we ate, it was time for our annual baseball game. My dad and uncles against us kids.

"Batter up!" my dad called out as my cousin Billy stepped up to home plate. Lucky he was on our team. He could hit anything. When he was out at field, he'd leap into the air and make impossible catches. "That kid can jump higher than a cow's back!" our uncles used to say.

First pitch out, Billy hit the ball so hard, it clean disappeared. We thought we saw lightning as it hit the sky. Maybe the lightning was on its way. Was that what Gramma was going to catch in a jar?

"I'm going to be a Detroit Tiger someday," Billy said that day. We all knew that he most certainly would.

Next it was time for croquet, the biggest game of the day, which our uncles kept interrupting with friendly quarrels about bent hoops, crooked wickets and wanting to take reshots.

We had bag races, watermelon-seed-spitting contests, and rides on Grampa's draft horse, too. Until Grampa waved a yardstick in the air.

All of us kids dropped what we were doing and ran to the milk shed. We knew it was time to get measured. We did this every year.

I liked looking at the marks of my gramma and her sisters and brothers on the same doorway. Some shorter than mine. Hard to imagine that once they were little just like me.

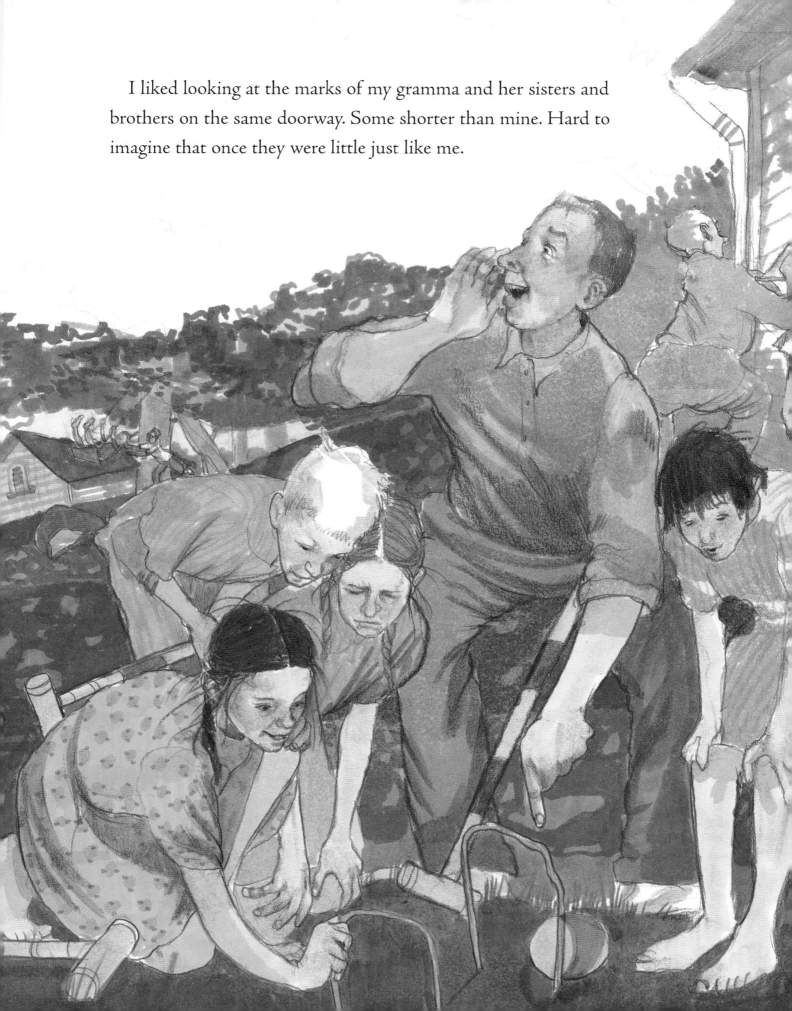

Aunt Bertha had gone to the house and fetched all the family portrait albums. The aunties showed us old brown photos and pointed. That was their father, who saved souls as a circuit preacher when he wasn't farming. Look, there were their favorite horses. Their eyes sparkled when they showed us their wedding pictures—the aunties were all married in their mother's parlor.

I watched Gramma to see if she would summon the lightning from the sky.

"It's time for our family photo!" Aunt Ivah called out as she jumped up and grabbed her camera. We kids didn't like this part because it meant that any dirt on our faces would be scraped off with a hankie that our aunties had spit on. Especially mine. "Everybody smile," Aunt Ivah sang out.

After this, the kids started to chant: "Stories! Stories! Stories, pleeeeeeeeze!"

Gramma and her sisters and brothers started quiet and slow. Uncle Ernest told about milking cows faster than lightning. Gramma told about how she and her sisters walked seven miles to a one-room schoolhouse over in Locke Center. And how each of them taught in that same school.

Then there was some quiet as Aunt Ivah started fanning herself. We knew she was getting ready.

"I remember the day I was driving the rig home from school, when I came upon . . . a real rattlesnake!"

We all looked at one another. Rattlers weren't around these parts, so we knew this was going to be good. "That thing was all coiled up and shaking its tail. Not a rattling sound, something more like a loud buzz. Belle horse just stood there and shook."

"What did you do, Aunt Ivah?" we asked.

"Well, sir, I stepped out of the buggy, took my umbrella and put it smack in the middle of that snake all coiled up. It just wrapped around that umbrella. I knew if it struck me, I was a goner." We all leaned forward.

"So I picked it up, gave the umbrella a sharp jerk, and flung that snake into Cecil Potter's field! Then I jumped into my buggy and galloped home—like the wind!"

All of my aunts and uncles laughed. Then a flicker of heat lightning sprang out of the horizon.

The air didn't move. Was some magic going to happen?

Aunt Adah fluttered her fan. We knew she was getting ready to top Aunt Ivah's story. "Have I ever told you children about the time I took a ride in the first newfangled motorcar in this here county?"

"Nooooooo!" we kids sang out.

"Well, sir, it belonged to Eldie Dunkle. My pa didn't approve of him no never, no how. 'He's a wild kid,' he'd rave. 'Don't never want to see you with the likes of him!'

"Then one day when I was walking home from prayer meeting, he rolled up next to me driving the shiniest machine I'd ever seen."

Aunt Adah stopped and fanned some more.

"What happened, Aunt Adah?" we begged.

"Well," Aunt Adah crowed, "I climbed right into that thing. Eldie shifted that contraption, making a terrible sound, and that roadster almost leapt right out from under us. It went so fast, my hat blew clean off. We were going almost forty miles an hour! We raced up Moyer Road, hurtled around Evie Peters' barn, almost flattened the Bender sisters' fruit stand, then howled down Dietz Road!"

We gasped.

"And when we skidded to a stop in front of Pa's barn, there he was, just a-standing there." She stopped again and fanned herself.

"What did he do, Aunt Adah? What happened?" we all pleaded.

"Not a blessed thing!" she answered, and laughed so hard, she almost dropped her lemonade.

Heat lightning flickered again. There was a low rumble of thunder off in the distance.

Now I watched my grandmother. She smiled and gave me a wink. It was her turn.

"Well, sir," Gramma began, "I was but a girl, out plowing, helping Pa with the fields—his team could pull those rows straight as an arrow—when the team reared and bolted and dragged me halfway down the field before I could free myself! When I stood up, there was a fierce and clattering roar in the sky above me."

We all leaned toward her.

"It was like thunder and fierce lightning!"

She stopped and sipped her lemonade.

"What was it, Gramma?" we kids begged. I looked up, waiting for the lightning.

"Well, sir, I couldn't believe what I was seeing above me."

We crawled close to her knee.

"There, like a giant dragonfly, with two sets of wings, growling and roaring, pitching and rolling, spewing foul-smelling smoke . . ." She leaned forward. "It was the first-ever flying machine in the state of Michigan!" We all clapped with delight.

That would have been a perfect time for the lightning to come. But it didn't, and it was almost dark. I whispered to Gramma, "What about the lightning in a jar?"

She adjusted her glasses and gave me a look. "Have the last rays of sun left the grass?" she asked.

I looked real hard. "Yes," I said.

"Then sit down, child."

Aunt Bertha brought a wicker laundry basket full of glass canning
jars and set them at Gramma's feet.

"Many years ago, when your aunties and uncles and I were but
children, our grampa showed us what I am about to show you."

She leaned down and touched the grass, cupping something in her
hands. She thought for a moment and then said,

"Shadows lengthen, the day near done,
birds fly low at setting sun.
Stars will rise from earth below,
in these hands their light will glow.
Come up, lightning, come up, stars,
we'll snatch you up in these here jars!"

She blew into her hands and let something go. It flew for a
moment, then landed deep in the grass. We watched and watched,
but nothing was happening. Low thunder rumbled just above us.

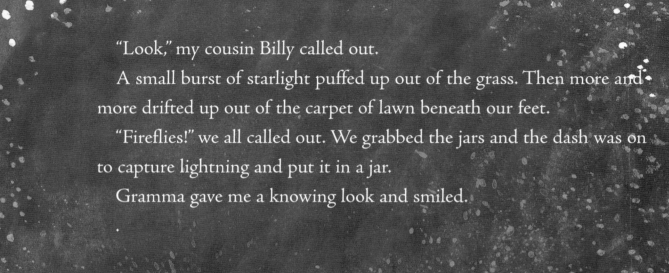

"Look," my cousin Billy called out.

A small burst of starlight puffed up out of the grass. Then more and more drifted up out of the carpet of lawn beneath our feet.

"Fireflies!" we all called out. We grabbed the jars and the dash was on to capture lightning and put it in a jar.

Gramma gave me a knowing look and smiled.

When everyone had gone home that night, Gramma and I sat on the porch swing together. We looked at the flickering jar. And even though fireflies are common in Michigan on summer nights, never had I seen so many as that night. And as long as I live I'll believe that somehow Gramma called them up—with her stories and her magic.

That night seems so long ago. But the reunion is here again. My family is arriving—now! My heart is racing.

We'll eat scrumptious Jell-O and meatloaf, play baseball and croquet, spit watermelon seeds, and scrawl new measurements on my milk house doorjamb. We'll look at photo albums; we'll laugh at some and cry at others. We'll remember the stories: how Gramma saw the first flying machine and Aunt Ivah conquered the rattler. We'll talk about Billy, and how he should have been a Detroit Tiger, but gave his life for his country in a war far away.

Then, when the sun is low and the shadows long, we'll all sit and fan ourselves in the shade of the maple trees. Only a new crop of children will gather at our knees. My father, my grandmother, my aunts and uncles are no longer here. So now it is we who must tell their stories and bring them back for fleeting moments.

Then I will show the children the magic that my gramma showed me. I'll call the stars from beneath their feet, and as they rise in the warm night air, these children will leap as high as a cow's back to gather them up.

I'll send them home with full bellies, tired bones and flickering jars in their laps. Their hearts will be overflowing. Full of lightning, put there by folks who loved them even before they were born. Gramma knew this well.

She also knew that someday they would tell their children about all of us, and of the magic nights when we caught lightning in a jar.